T0195845

Stephanie Bernard and Erika Francis

My Mom the PA

Illustrated by
Naira Julia Tangamyan

To order additional copies of this book, contact:
Xlibris
844-714-8691
www.Xlibris.com
Orders@Xlibris.com

ISBN: Softcover   979-8-3694-0626-7
            Hardcover   979-8-3694-0627-4
            EBook   979-8-3694-0625-0

Library of Congress Control Number: 2023916220

Print information available on the last page

Rev. date: 09/11/2023

This book is dedicated to
our families,
our work family at Shenandoah University,
and to all the PAs out there
making a difference in medicine!

My Mom's a PA
with a BIG role to play
She's a superhero
saving the day!

PAs are so smart
they study in school
PAs know a healthy
body is cool

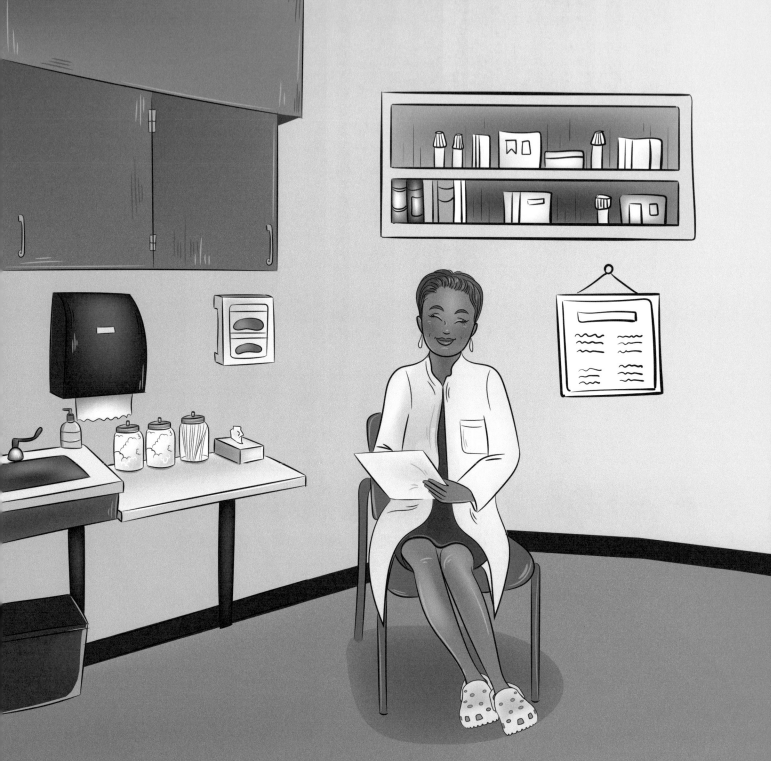

3

You'll find my Mom
in the clinic all day
Helping people feel better
in every way

4

My Mom the PA
wears a stethoscope, too
She listens to you
and knows just what to do

5

**My Mom the PA
will listen to lungs**

**She looks in your ears
and checks
under
tongues**

Sometimes my Mom
will give you a shot
She does it so quickly
it feels like a dot

8

My Mom the PA
listens to your heart
She makes sure you're healthy
right from the start

My Mom works as part
of a big healthcare team
When working together
they're living the dream

She teaches you how
to stay healthy and strong
Like eating less junk
and make exercise long

She's smart and she's kind
and she's always there
To listen and help
with a heart full of care

When medicines are
the thing that you need
She'll prescribe them for you
to feel better indeed

If you're feeling sick
and you need a hand
Just go see my Mom
she's got the plan!

PAs are the best
Go see one to know
They help you feel better
from head to toe

So next time you fall
or have a sick day
You know what to do
Go see the PA!

Printed in the United States
by Baker & Taylor Publisher Services